This book belongs to

There is nothing more fun than learning how to read.
Reading takes you on new adventures and helps you
learn new things. In a very special way, it's magical.
The people of British Columbia want to give you
the gift of reading as you prepare for school.

ACHIEVE BC

EDUCATION

BRITISH
COLUMBIA

www.gov.bc.ca

my animal friends

R. David Stephens

Illustrated by
Kathryn Shoemaker

VANCOUVER   LONDON

These are my animal friends.
They wake up with me and I wake up with them.

One says, "Cock-a-doodle-doo, cock-a-doodle-doo."
So what is it – a rooster or a kangaroo?
It says, "Cock-a-doodle-doo, cock-a-doodle-doo."

What is the name of my animal friend?

These are my animal friends.
They play with me and I play with them.

One says, "Bow, wow, bow-wow-wow."
So what is it – a dog or a goat or a sow?
It says, "Bow, wow, bow-wow-wow."

What is the name of my animal friend?

These are my animal friends.
They take care of me and I take care of them.

One says, "Moo, moo, moo-moo-moo."
So what is it — a cow or a kinkajou?
It says, "Moo, moo, moo-moo-moo."

What is the name of my animal friend?

These are my animal friends.
They follow me and I follow them.

One says, "Quack, quack, quackity-quack."
So what is it – a deer or a duck or a bat?
It says, "Quack, quack, quackity-quack."

What is the name of my animal friend?

These are my animal friends.
They sing to me and I sing to them.

One says, "Chirp, chirp, chirpity-chirp."
So what is it – a moose or a bear or a bird?
It says, "Chirp, chirp, chirpity-chirp."

What is the name of my animal friend?

These are my animal friends.
They sleep next to me and I sleep next to them.

One says, "Me-ow, me-me-ow."
So what is it – a frog or a cat or an owl?
It says, "Me-ow, me-me-ow."

What is the name of my animal friend?

These are my animal friends.
They love me and I love them.
They say, "Me-ow, bow-wow-wow,
moo-moo-moo and cock-a-doodle-doo."
They say, "Quackity-quack and chirpity-chirp."

They're my best friends on this earth!